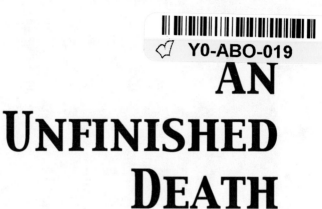

AN
UNFINISHED
DEATH

LAUREL DEWEY

THE
STORY PLANT

The Story Plant
The Aronica-Miller Publishing Project, LLC
P.O. Box 4331
Stamford, CT 06907

Cover design by Barbara Aronica-Buck
Author photo by Carol Craven

ISBN-13: 978-1-61188-004-5

Visit our website at www.thestoryplant.com

First Story Plant Paperback Printing: April 2011
Printed in the United States of America

1

Jane wasn't sure how long she'd been there, or how she got to this place. The last thing she remembered was finishing off a fifth of Jack Daniels with her younger brother, Mike. It was around 1:00 A.M. and they were still at her house after a three-day bender over the President's Day holiday weekend. As she recalled, she'd sucked the last drag of nicotine from her cigarette, crushed the empty pack and attempted a bank shot into the wastebasket across the room. But that was her last memory before she awoke into this odd scene.

There she was—sitting alone in a high-back wicker chair on a pristine, wraparound porch that extended out from what appeared to be one of those ancient Colorado sanitariums where people went to recuperate from TB or pneumonia. She looked down at her clothes, expecting to see a hospital gown to go along with the clinical setting. Instead, she wore her standard blue jeans, poplin shirt, leather jacket, and roughout cowboy boots. She could feel the butt of her Glock biting into her rib cage. She swore she'd been clad in her Denver Broncos sweatshirt and sweatpants just minutes before catapulting into this unsettling shift in scenery.

Good God. In all her years of heavy drinking, Jane had never hallucinated. And now, here she was—right in the middle of one hell of a disturbing delusion that felt a little too real.

She noted how heavy her hands felt against the wicker armrests. Her feet, in turn, hung like lead on the white-planked porch. As she gazed forward, she suddenly noticed the exquisite expanse of trimmed grass that seemed to roll for miles into the aqua sky. The air smelled sweet, like spring when life in Colorado comes alive after months of winter's death and dormancy. The scent of blooming lilacs and sweet daffodils created an intoxicating perfume that calmed and caressed her senses.

Not 40 feet in front of Jane, a lone East Indian in his mid-forties unexpectedly appeared in the middle of the grass. He stared at her for a minute before cocking his head to the side and waving. She told her body to stand up, but somehow the message didn't reach the correct part of her brain because she stayed inexplicably frozen to the wicker chair. The man climbed the seven steps that led to the porch and rested his lean body against the railing in front of her. The persistent woody scent of sandalwood enveloped him, an outward signature that seemed to herald his appearance. His smile was warm and genuine, his demeanor gentle and kind.

"Jane...Jane Perry?" he stated, almost as if he was reading her name on an invisible card that floated above her head.

Jane nodded. For some reason, speaking was difficult. The heaviness grew more profound in her body. *What in the hell is happening?*

He extended his hand. "Devinder Bashir." Jane lifted her leaden hand off the armrest and shook his hand. He held onto it, his grasp reading her thoughts. "How very odd," Devinder said in a faraway tone.

Jane tensed. She struggled to force out two words. "What's odd?"

"You still have the weight of the world." His eyebrows furrowed. "You're not dead yet."

Jane slammed back into her thirty five-year-old, aching body. She opened her eyes and sat up in bed. "Holy Shit!" she sputtered, her heart racing. Her Denver Broncos shirt was soaked in acrid sweat. Pressing her palm to her forehead, she attempted to assuage the relentless throbbing that bore into her skull. Jane felt halfway outside of herself, as she rolled off her bed and stumbled down the hallway to the living room. She found her brother, Mike, on the couch. He was right where she had left him just five minutes before. But a quick glance of the clock showed that five hours had passed. *This makes no damn sense.* Jane steadied herself on the kitchen counter, while another wave of excruciating pain rippled across her temples. This was unlike any hangover she'd ever experienced.

"You're not dead yet," the Indian man who called himself Devinder Bashir told her.

"Yet," Jane whispered, as an uneasy shock traversed her spine.

Is this even real? she questioned herself. *Or is this a freakish extension of the dream?*

She lunged toward her sleeping brother, impatiently tugging on his shirt. He stirred briefly before starting to turn away, but Jane pulled him back toward her. "Mike! Wake up! Goddamnit! Wake up!"

Mike grimaced. He unhinged one eye to focus. "What the fuck time is it, Janie?"

"Six o'clock."

"Fuck me. Wake me up at 11:00."

Jane grabbed his shoulders with urgency, shaking him. "Mike! Wake the fuck up!"

Now, he was pissed. Well, as pissed as Mike Perry could be—which was more like what bothered looked like with most people. "What, Janie?"

"Slap me."

"I don't wanna slap you."

"Mike, I'm not kidding. I need you to slap me." Mike made a weak attempt that resembled brushing a hair off his sister's face rather than a smack. "Fuck," Jane mumbled, still feeling outside of her body. "Mike, I mean it, if you don't slap me hard, I'm cutting off your beer!"

That got his attention. He landed a good cuff across his sister's left cheek.

Jane shook off the sting and let out a satisfied breath. "Okay. I'm not dead."

"You're not dead?" Mike sat up. "Jesus, Janie. If you're geeked up on meth, at least cut me in on some."

"I'm not doing meth, Mike! It interferes with my job description."

"Could've fooled me, Detective. What time is it again?"

Jane sensed the unfinished seam of another reality that was still wide open. "Time for a drink."

2

After an uneventful night of dreams, Tuesday morning arrived. Jane knocked back a breakfast of three cups of coffee, four cigarettes and a two-day old chocolate donut. As she drove to Denver Headquarters, she could remember every moment of the dream. It still shook her core with the same uneasy shudder. To her knowledge, she'd never had a dream where a complete stranger introduced himself by his full name. Devinder Bashir. How in the hell did her subconscious invent that foreign name? Must have read it on a homicide victim list, she reasoned. Then again, she hadn't worked a homicide with an East Indian vic or family member in years. Logic, use logic, she urged herself, while she lit a new cigarette off the dying ember of another. It was the booze, she decided. Yeah, that made the whole thing easier to swallow. At 35, her weather-beaten body was getting too old for three-day binges where incoherency was the objective. Drowning out the voices was always the goal, achieving that place of numbness where she could stare into the void and feel nothing. It was taking longer to get to that empty space and, once there, the sweet peace lasted less and less time. All addicts eventually slammed against this wall. At this point, one either got help or dove deeper into the bottle. Jane figured that she could still swim pretty well, which made the latter option her preferred choice.

Just past 8:45 A.M, she peeled her 1966 ice blue Mustang into the parking garage on 13th and Cherokee. She finished off her sixth cigarette of the morning, as she walked to the elevator. After a three-day holiday weekend, she wondered how many people who had a pulse last Friday had given up the ghost by Monday night at the hands of another; people who had every good intention of seeing another week of existence, never seeing their sudden demise on the horizon. No sooner did that thought cross her mind when she heard Devinder's voice clearly. "You're not dead, yet."

"Jane!"

She spun around. Detective Bruce Miles was walking toward her. He'd worked vice and narcotics for more than 20 years and it showed on his grizzled face. Miles was less than a year from retirement and had started to slow down. Cops called guys like Miles "slugs" or "hairpieces," insinuating that they were just going through the motion and had lost their investigative edge. Jane couldn't figure out how anyone could handle dealing with prostitutes, child pornography, hardcore druggies and all of the gutter swine that accompanied the vice gig. Years before, before she scored a slot in homicide, she had had her fill working assault and dealing with battered kids and drug-addled women. After 20 years of working with filth, she understood why Miles wasn't as connected to the job as he used to be. She also sensed that he bent his elbow to the breaking point at "choir practice" with the same passion and frequency as she did.

"Nothin' like a three-day weekend to fuck up your Tuesday mornin'," Miles grumbled.

"Catch a case this early?"

"Yeah. Suicide on Saturday night. Guy swallowed an Ambien, Valium, Oxycodone and whiskey cocktail."

"Since when did suicide become a vice?"

"When you're layin' butt naked amidst your child porn collection when you kick."

Jane tried to erase the disturbing image from her mind. "Fuck. You get all the choice cases, don't you?"

Miles lit a cigarette. "This one's got one of those added complications to make it even more interesting."

"What's that?"

"A cultural taint."

Jane was somewhat aware of the stigma that stained a family when suicide occurred and the various superstitions that proliferated, especially in the more upper crust Middle Eastern bloodlines. "Muslim?" she asked.

"Nah," Miles flipped open the file. "This guy is from the rice and curry crowd. Wealthy East Indian importer."

Jane's throat tightened. "What…what's his name?"

Miles glanced at the page. "Devinder Bashir."

It isn't possible. That's what Jane kept saying to herself, as Miles walked away and got into his Buick. No, no, this is a dream now. But no matter how many times Jane pinched, slapped and poked herself, she didn't wake up. Be rational, she counseled herself, as she tried to reconcile the distorted thoughts racing through her mind. But there was nothing rational about this.

Nor was Jane's next move. Instead of heading upstairs to her third floor homicide office, she ducked back into her Mustang and followed Miles out of the parking garage.

It took three cigarettes to reach the upscale neighborhood in Cherry Creek, where the grieving widow Bashir resided. In some ways, Jane was surprised that Miles didn't see her tailing him. Then again, he wasn't the sharpest tool in the cop shed as of late. She parked the Mustang behind a large truck on the opposite side of the street and watched as Miles lumbered over to a thirty-something, blonde Caucasian woman watering her lawn. They shook hands before she led him into the sprawling two-story McMansion.

Jane lit another cigarette and mused over Devinder Bashir choosing a blonde, white chick as his wife. Jesus, she ruminated, she must have been some catch for him to marry outside his culture. Maybe she's one of those white women who likes to meditate and chant, burn incense, listen to zither music, use Ayurvedic herbs, and can't get enough Bollywood film classics? Devinder's mother must love this cross-cultural union. Then, once again, the memory of the dead man manifesting to her in a booze-induced dream reared its ugly head. That distorted sensation of standing outside her body swelled around her and was about to rattle her cage when she saw a rough-looking, Caucasian male emerge from the house's three-car garage. He looked to be in his mid-twenties, well built and physically fit. The guy wore a tool belt, which he appeared to be well acquainted with. While Jane observed him from afar, over the next 20 minutes, he went about changing sprinkler heads on the lawn, securing the rain gutter over

the garage and doing a host of other sundry jobs. He continued to work when Miles re-emerged from the house,
followed by Mrs. Bashir. She walked Miles down the brick
lane that led to the street, shook his hand solemnly, and
brushed her golden locks away from her grief-stricken face.

Jane watched her turn away and motion to the fellow
with the tool belt. In that same moment, Miles lowered his
tired body into his Buick and surreptitiously removed a
flask from the inside pocket of his jacket.

"Oh, Jesus, Miles," Jane whispered. It wasn't a derision
of judgment; it was more about a code of ethics. Even
though Jane could drink Miles under the table, she'd always waited until 5:00 P.M. to do it. This guy needs to
hang up his shield and soon.

Miles drove away and Jane was just about to follow
when she saw a flicker of body language between the
mournful widow Bashir and the workman. It suggested
a more familiar than professional relationship. The way
she tilted her head, and the way he relaxed, leaning his
taut body toward hers. But it didn't take a body language
expert to read between the lines when she threw her head
back laughing, and he pulled her to his chest and passion-
ately kissed her.

Okay, Jane thought, the woman's husband had just
suicided three days earlier, butt naked and surrounded by
his secret stash of kiddie porn. Shit, it just didn't get more
shameful and disturbing than that. But instead of show-
ing a certain amount of appropriate emotion, the widow
chose to play tonsil hockey with her blue-collar toy.

3

As Jane pulled back into the parking garage at Headquarters, she realized that the blonde widow had no clue that anyone had been watching her aroused antics once Detective Miles had beat feet. Up to that point, she'd played her role with the exact degree of tempered sadness. Did Devinder learn of this illicit affair and was that what drove him to OD? Did Devinder's lust for child porn drive his widow into another man's arms? Do these two questions sound like bad daytime drama schlock? Jane's head swirled with the various scenarios, as she headed upstairs to homicide.

She got off the elevator on the third floor and saw Detective Miles walking away from the vice division. Jane made a split-second decision and headed straight for Miles' cubicle. Once there, she scanned his disheveled desk for any sign of plastic-covered evidence materials or photos of Devinder's suicide. Under a stack of files, she found the color photos she was looking for. There he was, sprawled naked across his bed amidst a myriad of magazines and photographs, nude children posed in sexually compromising positions. Jane quickly looked at the establishing shot of the scene before turning her attention to the close up of his left hand holding the handwritten suicide note. Jane could clearly make out the short, three-sentence note:

My secret haunts me.

I can no longer hide from it.

I have shamed my family name and now I must die for my mortal sins.

Jane looked back at the establishing shot of the death scene. Something wasn't right. The pornography was not as much scattered as it appeared. In fact, it looked almost like…

"Jane?"

She was so deep in thought, she didn't hear Miles return, fresh coffee in hand.

Miles looked perplexed. "Can I help you with something?" he asked, an undercurrent of irritation bleeding through.

Jane put down the photo. "You know, uh…" She stalled. "I thought I knew this guy. Bashir? Uh, an old case from way back. A perp…" Jane realized she was babbling. Miles regarded her with a suspicious eye. "But, it's not the same guy." She ducked out of his cubicle and turned down the hall toward homicide, wondering whether she looked as crazy as she felt right then.

4

Chris Crawley, Jane's partner—both on and off the job—wanted to come over that night, but Jane told him that she was meeting her brother. Chris bought the lie, although he fumed like a peevish schoolboy for an hour because he couldn't get what he really wanted. Jane wasn't in the mood to deal with Chris, knowing that his main objective was to get laid and then pass out half drunk somewhere between her couch and the bed. Chris had always been a boor, but his behavior in and out of the bedroom had become gradually more aggressive. The sex had gone from moderately rough to excessively rough, depending on the amount of booze each of them had consumed. Right now, Jane wanted to be alone with her weary mind and notch another night with no anomalous dreams.

After a dinner of microwave macaroni and cheese and a can of peas, Jane finished her sixth Corona and still felt on edge. She poured a shot of Jack Daniels and then another shot. She sought that sweet spot of numbness, and it took two more shots of Jack to travel there. She fell back onto her bed, free-floating in the comforting haze. Reaching the center point between all of the past pain and all of the trauma that was yet to unfold, she allowed the booze to dictate her descent into the stillness where she could forget who she was and all she would never become. It was so quiet and peaceful that she didn't even feel herself slide under the thin veil that shielded this world from the next.

She opened her eyes and found herself back on the same white-planked porch, sitting in the same wicker chair within the same scene as before. Devinder was leaning on the same railing. He looked within her. That familiar signature scent of sandalwood perfumed the air around him, causing Jane to feel a strange sense of calm and protection. The only difference between this scene and the last was the appearance of many more people in the general area, both on the porch and around the extensive grassy landscape that seemingly swept for miles. The heaviness of Jane's body returned like an anchor weighting down her soul.

"How did I get back here?" she asked Devinder, each word an effort.

"When you drink, you detach from your physical body which leaves you open to any number of unwelcome journeys," Devinder stated in his lilting eastern tongue. "Although I don't like the fuel it took to get you here, I am glad you came back." He smiled, warmly and genuinely. It was as if he knew how difficult it was for Jane to speak. "It'll be easier if you just think what you wish to say. I'll hear you much better."

Jane's first thought was that Devinder was half-cocked. Then suddenly, she clearly heard his voice without seeing his lips moving.

"If I'm half-cocked," he said, grinning, "then what does that make you?"

"Shit," Jane uttered, with no heaviness attached to it and without any timbre coming from her vocal chords. "I can hear you." Jane noticed that she could move her hands off the wicker chair more easily and that a modicum of lightness enveloped her. "Is this a dream?"

"What do you think?"

"I think that in a dream when you look into someone's eyes, they're flat with no past, present or future behind them."

"And now, when you look into my eyes, are they flat?"

Jane saw the three-dimensional pulse behind Devinder's eyes. "No."

"So, given your criteria, this is no dream."

"And given the fact that your name is on the board at Headquarters…" Jane felt her heart sink.

Devinder moved from the railing to a wicker chair beside Jane that seemed to appear out of nowhere. He turned the chair, so he was facing her. "You're not supposed to be here, Jane. Your light is too bright." Devinder gestured with his left hand to the back of Jane's neck, pulling her hair away and revealing a pinpoint shaft of brilliant white light that shone like a precise radar beam. "Mine is much less," he offered, turning down his shirt collar. A dimmer beacon of light jetted from his neck. "It's the last connection we have with the physical reality that we leave behind. The closer we get to the next level of transformation, the weaker the light becomes. When we accept that we are dead, we are truly free and homeward bound."

Jane looked out at the people milling on the porch and lawn. To her, it looked like a disjointed Bergman film. The divergent assortment of souls was evident—everyone from a farmer in overalls and a pinstripe-suited executive to a toddler playing with a beach ball and a rough-looking biker. Each had the same pinpoint of light emanating from the back of their neck, with varying degrees of illumination.

Devinder explained to her that a soul only comes to this place when a person dies suddenly, violently, or isn't ready to accept his or her demise. "We have a ninety-eight-year-old woman upstairs who still can't believe she's dead," he said, shrugging of his shoulders. Jane noticed that the little girl with the beach ball had the least amount of light coming from her neck. Devinder read her thoughts. "She's almost ready to transition to the next level. Pretty soon, we'll look over there and she'll be gone."

Jane ran her fingers through her hair. "So what in the hell am I doing here?"

"Perhaps…so you can help me?"

"Help you what?"

"Remove the shame of my death."

Jane felt a jolt of judgment. "Hey, I can't change history. You're the one who chose to get naked, cover yourself in kiddie porn and chase three bottles of drugs with a bottle of whiskey."

Devinder held Jane's hand tightly in his left hand. "You know I didn't do that, Jane."

Jane looked into his eyes. She could see the truth. And in a split second, she saw the crime against Devinder manifested before her…

Devinder is relaxing on his living room couch, reading. His pretty wife with the flowing blonde hair brings him a glass of water into which she has crushed five tablets of Ambien and five tablets of Valium. He fights sleep, but finally succumbs to it, as his wife watches from the kitchen. She checks his pulse and then walks quickly to the front door, opens it and ushers in a person. The twenty-something worker appears, carrying a large bag. The two of them lift Devinder off the couch and carry him into the master bedroom. His wife exits briefly, as the young stud opens his large bag and brings out one hideous photo and magazine after another of child pornography. He strips Devinder of his clothes and then carefully arranges the collection of porn around his nude body.

The wife then reappears with a bottle of whiskey, three orange prescription bottles and a large envelope. She pours a tall glass of whiskey into a bedtime water glass and dissolves ten tablets each of Ambien, Valium and Oxycodone into the amber liquor. Once satisfied with the mixture, the young man pulls Devinder's unconscious body up to a sitting position and pries open his mouth. The wife pours in the fatal concoction. Devinder gags but the young man manipulates his throat little by little to encourage the drugged man to swallow. Ten minutes later, the deadly brew is drained. They drop his body back onto the bed and the wife takes what is left in the whiskey bottle, dripping it over her husband's face and chest before laying the bottle next to his body.

She puts on a pair of latex gloves, reaches into the large envelope the young man brought, withdraws a handwritten note and slides it between the fingers on Devinder's left hand. Reaching back into the envelope, she removes a pen and places it next to his body. The young man amends the placement by putting the pen into Devinder's right hand. The three orange prescription bottles positioned next to his body completes the fabricated suicide.

They wait in silence, as Devinder's body begins to spasm, and foam appears around the edges of his mouth. They hold him down, as the wife pinches off his nostrils with her red acrylic fingernails. The spasms continue in violent waves until they finally stop. She checks his pulse. "Nothing." She stands up and pulls the young man toward her, with a look of conquest and wicked seduction. In turn, he hungrily kisses her, ripping off her shirt. They fall into the Indian rug at the foot of the bed, blinded by hedonistic rage, devouring each other like wild animals after a good kill…

Jane felt physically sick and turned away from Devinder. Looking out toward the grassy expanse, she spotted the toddler with the beach ball. The little girl stared at Jane, smiled and then dissolved into thin air.

"I can't do that yet," Devinder stated, acknowledging the child's ascent.

Jane turned to Devinder. "Why did she kill you?"

"I loved Cath deeply. Cath deeply loved my money."

Cath? Jane thought. Who the fuck calls themselves Cath?

Devinder read her thoughts. "It's short for Catherine."

"Not catheter, huh? What happened to divorce?"

"My family is Hindu and extremely traditional. We are devout in our beliefs. No drinking. No smoking. No divorce."

"No fun for her," Jane intoned. "I guess whatever drew her to you—whatever exotic allure you triggered in her—wore off."

"My family's import business has always been time-consuming. I traveled a lot to India on buying trips. She used to come with me. I used to buy her the most expensive sandalwood incense on the market. It would linger in the air for hours after it was extinguished. When she told me she wasn't interested in joining me on my trips, I told her to burn the sandalwood. That way, she could remember me when I was gone."

"But she found something more alluring than sandalwood to occupy her time when you were away, right?"

"Yes." He responded, without a hint of hatred.

"Why do you accept it?"

"Because I accept my karma. When I was alive, I lived with an honest heart, devoted to my family and honoring my wife. I sought my salvation through good deeds and self-control, as any good Hindu would."

"Excuse me, Devinder, but you're a fucking saint. If I was in your shoes, I'd be sitting up here looking for someone to cap the worthless slut."

"Bad karma, Jane."

So she wanted out, Jane thought. But there's no life insurance paycheck from suicide. Devinder looked at her and she clearly understood Cath's plan and expectations. A cultural taint. Detective Miles used that term when he first mentioned the suicide to Jane. The white woman feels constricted by the conventions of the exotic culture she probably thought was one long tantric orgy and then decides to use those conventions to her favor. Should call it a cultural shakedown.

"My soul won't rest," Devinder stated, the aroma of sandalwood thickening the air as he leaned toward Jane. "And my family will forever bear the shame of my death. It will kill my mother years before her time." He gently grasped Jane's hand. "Is it possible that you have been sent to me to save my soul?"

"I'm a cop, not a priest."

"I don't need a priest. I need a cop. A good cop. If you can show my death for what it was, you can lift the shame and I can accept my karma and my fate, and move on." Devinder's eyes dimmed with concern. "But you have miles of trouble."

Jane considered the obstacle of Detective Miles. Miles of trouble made sense. But she also understood something else.

Devinder moved his left hand to Jane's neck and pulled her hair away, exposing the pinpoint light. "It's getting dimmer, Jane. You're in danger."

5

Jane startled awake, shocked to find that it was already 8:00 A.M. on Wednesday. She remembered everything—especially Devinder's ominous warning. Bolting out of bed, she quickly showered and grabbed her morning coffee. She didn't think through what she was about to do because she knew that if she did, she'd be smart and reconsider the idea. The whole while, she had to keep in mind that a dead man was orchestrating this case.

Just after 9:00 A.M., she rolled to a stop in front of Mrs. Bashir's opulent home in Cherry Creek. A Range Rover was parked in the driveway. Jane walked up the driveway and checked the temperature of the SUV's hood. In the old West, law enforcement checked the heat of the dying coals from the criminal's campfires. In the modern world, one checked the heat of a suspect's hood to determine approximately how long the vehicle had been parked. Based on Jane's seasoned sense of hood temp, she figured the SUV had been there no longer than 30 minutes.

She walked around the Range Rover, scanned the windows and noted some movement in the kitchen inside the house. Carefully crawling amidst the perfectly manicured shrubbery, Jane peered inside. There was Cath looking grave and grim, surrounded by what Jane deduced were Devinder's truly grieving parents. The mother did indeed look frail, as if her world had crashed around her and she couldn't see clear of the debris to escape. She stayed quiet, as her husband appeared to make what looked like emotional appeals to Mrs. B. The blonde vixen hung her head, wiping away the occasional counterfeit tear, while she cupped her forehead in her hand. The father moved briefly out of Jane's point of view before reappearing at Cath's side, hand outstretched with what was obviously a check.

Cath turned away, even motioning with her crocodile-tear-stained hankie, as if she were saying, "No, please. I just couldn't accept that money!" But after the father pursued the matter with more vigor, Cath gave in and took the check. As Cath turned away, she caught sight of Jane framed in the window. Her mien changed from heartache to irritation, as she excused herself and crossed to the kitchen door.

"Can I help you?" Cath's voice was huskier than Jane imagined.

Jane quickly flashed her shield. "Detective Jane Perry," she stated with all the cop bravado she could rally at nine in the morning. "I knocked on your front door," Jane lied, extricating herself from the shrubs, "but I guess you couldn't hear." She peered over Cath's shoulder, trying to get a better look at Devinder's parents.

Cath closed the door, obviously wanting to keep her conversation with Jane private. "Detective Miles made no reference to you working this case."

"Really? Humph. That's odd. There's a gaggle of us down at Headquarters assigned to your husband's case…"

"A gaggle? What in the hell are you talking about?" She tossed her blonde locks over her shoulder and moved closer to Jane. Based on Jane's first real world impressions—as opposed to the disincarnate visions of Cath killing her husband and then engaging in carnal sex with her hump of a boy toy—this was a woman who spent most of her time between the Pilates center and the day spa. Her toned body was lean and her tanned skin polished to perfection. Under the conservative white tunic, Jane spied a pair of tits that stationed a little too upright for her 40-something age.

"Detective Miles is lead on the case, but we all work different angles."

"Angles?" she questioned, her come hither voice sounding more like "back off." "There is only one issue and that is the child pornography my late husband shamed our family with." Suddenly, the grieving widow reappeared on cue, complete with her manufactured facial distortions that attempted to convey dishonor with a capital D. Jane half-wished she could arrest the bitch for bad acting.

"Right. The porn. Child porn," Jane deadpanned. "Doesn't get more shameful than that…"

"It's a curse, Detective Perry," Cath interrupted, deciding that it was time to school Jane on the facts. "Not only did my husband corrupt his family's bloodline, he made it so that I could no longer live in this beautiful home."

"Sorry? I don't follow."

"A wife can't live in the same place where her sick, twisted husband took his life. It's asking too much."

The pieces began to click in Jane's head. "Wow…and with a helluva real estate market these days. The house could be up for sale for six months and it still might not sell. Even then, you'd be lucky to get 60 percent of what you paid for it…"

"Fortunately, I don't have to worry about such things."

Now it was Jane's turn to exercise her acting chops. "How's that?"

"My in-laws are very generous and understand my delicate situation."

Without realizing it, Cath exposed part of the personal check in her hand. Jane furtively glanced down and saw a four followed by six very nice zeros. Even during the booming days of Colorado real estate, this tony mini-manor wasn't worth that much. Jane reckoned the additional amount was for Mrs. B.'s pain and suffering. Consider it a little somethin'-somethin' to take the edge off the shame.

Jane peered over Cath's shoulder. "You know, we don't have any interviews with your late husband's parents. I'd love to talk to them…"

"Are you crazy?" The sexual barracuda had been replaced by an all-business broad. "They are beyond distraught. This whole thing came out of nowhere! None of us expected it! And besides, Detective Miles promised me that there would be no tasteless follow-up with the investigation."

Tasteless, Jane thought. Not a word Miles bandies around. Jane knew that what Cath really meant was that she had it on good faith by her good ol' broken down, over-the-hill, alcoholic, vice cop that this purposely prurient, suicide set-up would stay confined to the walls of

Denver Headquarters and not bleed into too many departments that might leak this deviant case to the media. Yeah, that would just fuck up everything, Jane reasoned. Even psychopaths such as Mrs. B. knew that if the local press picked up this story, her life would be one flame eater away from a circus. No, deep scrutiny was not wanted here. Better to take the dirty money, meet your trashy, 20-something fleabag with six-pack abs outside the county line and disappear into obscurity.

Jane's expression must have concerned Cath because if Jane read the double-D tramp's body language correctly, she was exhibiting a threatening stance.

"I think you need to leave, Detective Perry." Cath took another purposeful step toward Jane, her Botoxed forehead unable to show the true scorn she really felt at that moment. "I don't need this to get complicated."

Jane stared into Cath's eyes. She wished thoughts were as transparent as they were in the middle world with Devinder. But even though she couldn't hear Cath's thoughts, she could patently feel them. It was the stuff that raised the hair on your arms and sent a jolt down your spine. You can't hear the threat but your body reacts just the same. This is one desperate woman, Jane surmised. And nothing was going to complicate her plan at this critical juncture.

Jane held Cath's gaze a little longer. She could outlast anybody in a stare down and she'd perfected the intimidating narrowing of her eyes to complete the menacing effect. Finally, Jane nodded, wished Mrs. B. a nice day and walked back to her Mustang. But on her way there, she couldn't help but see something sitting at the curb— something that could be important. When Cath returned inside, Jane quickly collected the evidence. She had one more stop before going to Headquarters.

By the time Jane arrived back at Headquarters, she hoped she had enough to convince her boss, Sergeant Morgan Weyler, to take a hard look at Devinder's case. At least, she figured, she had something to cast doubt on the suicide. Right now, doubt was all Jane needed before Miles buttoned up the suicide and sent the merry widow on her way.

But Jane smelled trouble when she approached Weyler's office and saw Miles seated across the desk from her boss.

"What in the hell's goin' on, Jane?" Miles erupted. Jane could smell the booze on his breath.

"We got a call an hour ago from Devinder Bashir's widow," Weyler offered in his usual calming tone.

"Her exact words?" Miles interrupted with a sharp edge, "'Who's the bitch named Jane and why is that cunt coming to my house unannounced?'"

Jane was cornered. "Humph. Well, looks like I'm crossing her off the Christmas card list!"

Miles was dogged. "She also wanted to know why we had a gaggle of detectives workin' her case. I assured Mrs. Bashir that it was just me workin' the case. At least, I thought I was workin' it solo! Since when did homicide start hijackin' vice cases?"

"When the suicide is really a homicide." Jane let that gem linger in the air.

Weyler trusted Jane enough to wave off Miles' blustering indignation. "What proof do you have?" he asked.

Jane produced three orange prescription bottles. "I saw these through a clear plastic garbage bag at the curb of the Bashir's house. Trash is still open season, right?" Miles looked wary, but Weyler nodded. "So, I took a look at them real closely. The date is almost one year ago and if you look at Devinder's name on the bottle…" Jane handed a bottle to each of the men, "you can see how the lettering was skillfully duplicated with a computer and literally pasted over the real owner of these drugs."

Miles lifted the tape to reveal Cath Bashir's name on the prescription bottle.

"I just came from that doctor's office," Jane continued. "It's a plastic surgeon. What a shock, right? Cath had a boob job and ass implants last year. They gave her Ambien to sleep, Valium to take off the edge, and everybody's favorite painkiller, Oxycodone. Apparently, she told the doc that she needed refills about three months after the surgery because of the continued discomfort when she sat, walked or took a breath!"

Miles looked shocked. "Patient records are confidential. You don't just walk in off the street with no warrant and get this info!"

"You know, it's just amazing the kind of things you can learn when you're a woman and you're talking to another woman and then you flash a badge and tell that woman that there are children in danger."

"Children?" Weyler questioned.

"That was a stretch, boss. But remotely, kids are involved. The porn part of this. Anyway, I've found that if you use the kid card, you've got a winning hand and a better chance at gaining info."

Miles' fury built. "Off the record, of course! That way, they don't lose their job for talking!"

"Well, yeah. But we build a case from here…"

"We?" Miles yelled. "Are there not enough homicides in Denver, that you gotta infringe on my territory?"

"Bruce," Jane stated, "Devinder Bashir was killed with premeditation."

"Who told you that?" Weyler asked.

Jane hesitated. "My gut tells me."

Miles threw up his hands. "The DA doesn't accept gut as evidence!"

"I'm telling you, he was killed by her tool of a boyfriend. They drugged Devinder and set up the scene to make it look as smarmy as possible. Devinder wasn't depressed. He didn't do drugs, or drink. It goes against his Hindu faith!"

"What the hell!" Miles mocked. "You act like this perv was your buddy!"

Jane's ire peaked. "Fuck it, Bruce! He's not a perv! He's a decent man with a good heart who got set up by his gold-digging, Botox bitch of a wife! I know him!" Jane realized she'd said too much. "I knew him," she quickly corrected. She turned to Weyler. "Boss, Devinder was killed. You gotta trust me on this one." She turned to Miles. "Check out the suicide note. Devinder is left-handed. It was written with a right-handed slant. The pen is in Devinder's right hand in the crime shot. Sloppy job on their end. And the note itself? It uses words that Devinder doesn't say. The last part…I have shamed my family name and now I must die for my mortal sins? Devinder is a devout Hindu. Hindus don't believe in mortal sin. They believe bad luck is due to bad karma. The person who really wrote this note should have used the word karma and it would have been more believable, but that person's not too bright. And I'm betting that the porn was downloaded by Cath's human dildo of a boyfriend. Get a warrant for the asshole's computer and you'll see the download history for yourself!"

"With nothin' to support any of this, except for your gut feeling!" Miles screamed, his face turning five shades of crimson. "I got less than a fuckin' year left on the job, Jane. I'm not gonna put my ass on the line without tangible evidence!"

"We have the drugs with the computerized name on the bottle!"

"Which will get thrown out of evidence by the DA because of your OTR interview."

"He's right, Jane," Weyler quietly agreed.

Now Jane needed a late morning adult beverage. She had to keep pushing the true numinous instigator of this investigation to the back of her mind and focus on the fact that her gut really did drive her actions. "So, that's it? You'll try to track down the porn, but you won't find anything on Devinder's computer and there'll be no credit card charges for overseas kiddie skin rags. And by the time the trail runs cold, Cath and her waste of skin scrote will have jumped five time zones, never to be seen again. Great. Fucking great!" She turned to Miles with one last appeal. "Take another look at the crime scene photos. It's hinky, Bruce. JDLR." Jane figured she might be able to create a pseudo bond with Miles by using cop talk. In this case, "JDLR" stood for "Just Doesn't Look Right." She wanted to say how the death scene was overkill in the smarmy department and to talk to Devinder's parents to find out about his recent behavior, any business troubles, depression—and so on. But it would have been like talking to a shoe and asking it to get up and walk.

After Miles left Weyler's office, Jane got the expected minor admonition from her boss, which she took with silent resentment. Later that morning, Chris successfully cornered her by the coffeemaker and offered Jane a take-out dinner on him that night. She was well aware that the dining destination would be her house and that dessert would be sex. Jane agreed with half-hearted desire. She'd have to pick up another bottle or two of Jack on the way home. She needed a few extra shots these days to tolerate Chris in bed.

6

"You gotta let it go, baby," Chris said to Jane, sliding his narrow frame behind her.

The Pad Thai was only partially eaten before Chris was already focused on dessert. Jane stood at the kitchen counter and grabbed the bottle of Jack she bought at the corner liquor store. She poured herself another tall shot. Is this shot number five or number six? She'd lost count after draining the six Coronas. Her body separated from her core and her mind wandered.

"You can't even tell me how you know Hindu Harry."

Chris' voice sounded distant. "Hindu Harry? You're a fucking riot," Jane slurred, dripping with sarcasm and knocking back the shot of booze.

"Baby, baby, baby," Chris' breath reeked of beer and whiskey, as he wrapped his arms around Jane's body from behind. He pulled her tucked shirt out of her pants with his usual lack of finesse and quickly worked his fingers under her bra.

Jane felt a jolt of heat rush down her spine. The booze was working fast tonight. Her mind flashed with split-second images. First, she saw her meeting with Cath Bashir earlier that day. Then, there was the unsuccessful appeal to Sergeant Weyler in his office. Next, she was buying the bottles of whiskey at the corner store. But then, within a millisecond flash, there was an unknown car behind her, as she drove home. What the fuck was that? Jane thought. She'd been so deep in her head that she hadn't paid her usual keen attention to her surroundings. That, and the fact that she'd already popped the cap off two beers in the car once she cleared the parking garage at Denver Headquarters.

Chris unbuttoned her jeans and forced his greedy hand into Jane's panties. Through it all, she was detached, becoming more of an observer than a participant. Her head spun, as the same split second images replayed again and again, always ending with her drive home and the lingering awareness that someone was behind her.

She felt Chris' hands remove her boots and jeans. Somehow, her bra and shirt fell off, as the room rotated in a chaotic whirl. She felt her naked back slam against the hallway wall and Chris' eager tongue brush against her teeth. His hot skin pressed against her breasts, as he held her arms above her head, pushing his thumbs hard into her wrists. Jane was pinned like a perp, playing out one of Chris' many sexual fantasies that always escalated in intensity. Jane's wrists began to throb where his thumbs were embedded and she used all of her waning strength to push him off of her body.

Stumbling down the hall to her bedroom, Jane broke free for only a few seconds before Chris grabbed her from behind and fell on top of her on the bed. The sexual fervor increased exponentially. Chris held Jane down with renewed strength. The more Jane fought to escape his dominating grip on her wrists, the more it excited him. His hot breath stung, as she felt him move down to her breasts. He dragged his teeth across her nipples and she winced. The bedroom spun faster. Jane tried to focus, but the severed sensation took over.

And then she felt nothing—no pain, no pressure, no fear. She closed her eyes, letting the liquor lead her to the empty place where time stood still.

"Jane." The voice was soft and familiar. "Open your eyes."

Jane didn't want to leave that sacred space of nothingness just yet. But she felt someone holding her hands gently, and it wasn't Chris.

She opened her eyes and found herself staring into Devinder's face. They were back on the white-planked porch, but they were alone this time. He turned over her wrists, revealing deep bruises. Speaking without voicing a word, he said, "This isn't love, Jane. Why do you let him hurt you?"

Jane felt paralyzed, unable to respond. Devinder softly reached behind her neck to expose the point of light. "It's growing dim, Jane. The danger is too close." Devinder's eyes looked over Jane's shoulder. "Behind you!" he screamed.

Jane crashed back into her body, her spine lifting off the bed in a brutal contraction. Disoriented, she turned around, throwing punches in the air behind her, but landing on nothing human. The bedroom was cloaked in darkness, save for the digital clock illuminated on the bedside table. 11:11. She swore that she and Chris had stood at the kitchen counter around 6:45 and that it wasn't much past that time when he started to peel off her clothes. She felt around in the bed for Chris, but he wasn't there. Putting her hand to her own body, she realized that she was naked. Something felt wrong—deadly wrong.

As Jane slowly lowered her frame onto the carpet and searched for clothing, there was still the sentient buzz from the booze. Touching her Denver Broncos sweatshirt and a pair of underwear, she quickly donned the garb. "Chris?" she whispered. No reply. "Chris?" she repeated with more urgency, her mouth like cotton. "Where the fuck are you?"

Suddenly, she heard a soft thump on her front porch. "Chris?" she implored. "Fuck!" Her heart raced. Is this real? She needed to look into someone's eyes to see if there was three-dimensional reality behind the orbs. She tried her best to shake off the buzz, as she crawled toward her bedside table. Carefully opening the drawer, she removed her Glock. She stood up and gradually made her way out of the bedroom and into the hallway that led a short distance to the living room. Hugging the wall, Jane held the Glock with both hands, nuzzle pointed toward the ceiling. Her breathing became shallow, as she desperately tried to perceive anything in the coal black darkness.

Thump! The sound distinctly came from the front porch. Is Chris so drunk and disoriented that he ended up outside after exhausting himself sexually? Jane crept cautiously to the front door. The only illumination in the living room was from the microwave oven clock that glowed green across the room. She checked the front door. It was locked but not dead-bolted. Yes, he could have easily staggered out onto the patio and locked himself out. It wouldn't be the first time.

Jane swung open the door, Glock relaxed at her thigh. "Chris," she said, with more irritation than fear. "Get your ass back in the house."

Out of the corner of her eye, she saw movement coming from the front of the house. Her heart raced. The damn buzz still compromised her perception. "Who's there?"

The sound of heels clicking on the cement pathway that led to Jane's house broke through the ebony stillness. Jane tensed.

"Jane Perry?"

Jane recognized the sultry voice of Cath Bashir. Cath flicked on a small sapphire flashlight. The violet light lit up the pathway and Cath's face with startling clarity. She observed Jane's abbreviated outfit with a slight smile. "Did I interrupt something?" she asked in a comfortable, relaxed cadence. She wore a heavy white coat with deep front pockets and blue jeans.

"How did you find where I live?" Jane said, feeling the air thick and tight around her.

"I followed you home from the police station. I figured you paid me an unexpected visit, so I owed you one." Cath moved a few feet closer to the steps that led up to the Jane's porch.

Yes. Right. Jane's muddled memory kicked into gear. There was somebody behind her when she drove home. In a weak attempt to remove the alcoholic residue that was clouding her acuity, Jane blinked hard. But the more she blinked, the more her perception became fractured.

"You're drunk," Cath declared, with a half-smile. "Is alcoholism a requirement for all Denver detectives? I mean, Detective Miles was half in the bag when he arrived at my humble abode." She smiled at the recollection. "You know, other people in my position would be really pissed off by that behavior, but I just figured I hit the jackpot."

Jane knew this was going in a bad direction. "Sure. Old addled, alchy cop is easy to mind fuck. Almost too easy, eh, Cath?" Jane heard herself slur her words. The Glock hung at her side and the thought crossed her mind that she wasn't sure if she removed the clip when she came home. She circumspectly rubbed her thumb against the bottom of the grip and sunk her finger into open space. No clip. But did I leave the lone round in the chamber, or did I eject it? Her memory was like Jell-o. Think, Jane, she screamed in her head.

Cath took another step toward her, stopping just shy of the bottom step. "I don't know why, Jane, but I feel like I can't trust you." The woman's voice was calm—way too calm.

The buzz prevented the oral censorship that Jane would normally choose at this point. "Funny. I feel the exact way about you. Too bad Devinder didn't see the light before you turned it off. You and your fucking dick of a boyfriend." Cath coolly stayed in place, looking up at Jane with absolutely no fear. "I wonder if the little prick is aware that when you tire of him, you'll chuck his sorry ass to the trash heap, too. I mean, like, actually in the trash. Can't leave a trail of co-conspirators, can you?"

"My gosh," Cath said with wide-eyed interest, "you really are perceptive, aren't you? But I don't think I can kill again. That's not to say it wasn't a rush." Cath's demeanor shifted. Her psychotic eyes glazed over, as they bored into Jane's soul. "I thoroughly enjoyed the preparation as much as the execution. Watching Devinder die was…like…the most powerful Kundalini arousal in my body. I've never experienced anything so dark and erotic at the same time." She tilted her head. "You know the funny thing, Jane? I utilized the meditative tenets of the Hindu faith to center myself and facilitate a positive and prosperous outcome…"

"Then I fucked it up." Jane stated, bringing the conversation back to some level of reality.

Cath chuckled. "Yes, then you fucked it up." Her throaty voice was a demented singsong.

Jane prayed to God at that point that she chambered a round in the Glock. She lifted the pistol, grasping it with both hands and aimed it square at Cath's forehead. "I'll blast your fucking third eye out of your head, bitch." Jane couldn't stop her hands from shaking. She was never this unsteady on the job. Of course, she wasn't drunk or surfing a buzz when she was on duty. She looked at Cath. There wasn't a hint of tension in her tanned face. Either she's high or she's certifiable—or maybe both?

"I don't think so, Jane," Cath said with an eerie calm.

Jane's splintered memory quickly focused on Devinder and how he looked over her shoulder and screamed, "Behind you!" Jane spun around just as a dark figure lunged at her from the left side. A rope quickly encircled her throat and dug hard into her larynx. She struggled for air, as the figure pulled her to the ground, tightening the rope into her flesh. Jane felt herself losing consciousness. For a split second, she saw Devinder on the porch pulling back her hair and telling her that her light was dimming. That image stoked something primal in her. Gasping for breath, she pointed the gun toward what she hoped was his groin and not hers, and pulled the trigger. The kick sent them both backward. The rope still pulled against her neck. She worried the numbness of the liquor was preventing her from feeling any pain from the gunshot. But then she felt the slow release of the assailant, as he fell backward unconscious on the porch.

Jane struggled for air, as she weakly pulled the rope off her head.

"What have you done to him?" Cath screamed in a frenzy, her coolness quickly gone. She shone her flashlight onto the porch and the growing puddle of blood that was pouring from her young lover's genitals. "What in the hell have you done?" Jane tried to get up, but the darkness spun around her each time she tried to stand. "You've ruined him!" Cath shrieked. "You've ruined him!" Cath dug her hand into her coat pocket, pulled out a small revolver and sprung up the stairs.

Just before Cath squeezed the trigger, another shot rang out from Jane's front door, nailing Cath in the thigh and sending her sprawling onto her stomach. She cried out in agony. The sapphire flashlight fell out of her other hand and rolled to a stop at the feet of the shooter.

Jane looked up through her hazy vision and saw Chris standing in the doorway, completely naked. He was looking as wobbly and half-drunk as Jane.

"Fuck," he said with a raspy edge. "Call 9-1-1. I need a drink."

7

The next day was a blur. Jane gave her statement to Sergeant Weyler, implicating both Cath Bashir and her lover boy in the death of Devinder Bashir , as well as the attempted murder of herself. Lover boy had a 24-hour guard posted outside of his ICU room at Denver Health. He told the cops—in a slightly higher octave than before—how Cath was the mastermind behind the murder of her husband. He turned on her faster than fish lying in the noonday sun. Lover boy spilled everything, including how she instructed him to write the suicide note and download the sickest child pornography he could find on his computer. Meanwhile, she handled the skillful computer match of the font on the prescription drug bottles, so she could create an exact duplicate of Devinder's name. The four million dollar check was returned to Devinder's parents who took some solace in the knowledge that their son had been set up and hadn't dishonored their family name.

Sergeant Weyler gave Jane the rest of the day off. She returned to her house around 4:00 P.M., exhausted and only functioning on a couple of cylinders. Collapsing onto her bed, she stretched like a tired cat and, in doing so, caught a glimpse of the insides of her wrists. Blue and green bruises the size of half dollars covered her skin. Her thoughts turned to the struggle on the porch, but then she realized that the bruises were the result of her activity with Chris from the night before. She'd survived plenty of rough days and nights in her life, and had her fair share of bloodied lips, noses and bruised ribs at the hands of another man. These new marks were just another reminder of why she started drinking 21 years ago. The bruises would disappear, but the reason Jane drank would remain in front of her, never allowing a moment's rest or a sense of safety. It was the pattern of belief that life and love were meant to be violent and painful. And thus, the pattern ensued of grabbing a bottle every time the twisted memory emerged of that fateful night when she was 14.

Patterns die hard. Jane was off the clock, so she didn't hesitate to locate a nearly empty bottle of Jack Daniels leaning against the bed and drain the final few shots from the bottle. Between the bone-breaking fatigue and the warm blanket of whiskey, she languidly collapsed on her bed, as her soul dove into that silent space.

The stale air of her bedroom disappeared, as she inhaled a blend of lilacs, spring daffodils and…sandalwood. Opening her eyes, she stared into the aqua sky and verdant grass. She felt the wicker chair against her back and then a gentle hand on her shoulder. Her body was so heavy—the weight of the world like a yoke around her waist. She tried to turn to him, but the movement was too difficult.

Devinder walked in front of her, his eyes warm and grateful. "Thank you, Jane."

She heard his voice clearly without his lips moving. Her head hurt and she felt a deep pressure she hadn't felt before in this place. "The light behind my neck," she asked, struggling with the words, even though she was speaking with her mind, "it's bright again?"

"No. Not completely," Devinder said.

"But I survived their attack."

"Yes, you did. But…" His eyes briefly looked off to the side.

"What?"

"I'm not certain. There's something else…very soon." He studied the white-planked porch floor. "There's a child…a little girl. She dies. Be careful, Jane."

Jane's chest tightened, as a blistering heat engulfed her left hand. "Tell me how to save her."

"You can't save her. It's her fate. Her karma."

"No! Tell me her name. She deserves a life."

"It's only one of her many lives, Jane. Just like the rest of us. I'll live again in a stronger body. But now, I need to rest and review." Jane noted that the light behind Devinder's neck grew much weaker. He took her hands in his. "You can take all the credit because you won't remember any of this."

"Of course, I will!"

"No. I promise you, you will not. And because you've never spoken a word of our meeting to anyone, there's no trail of the memory to others."

"I will remember you," Jane stressed.

Devinder smiled. "You won't. But I'll remember you. Forever." And with that, his image dissolved.

8

The next day, Friday, Jane sat at her desk waiting for Weyler to give her the heads up. The pressroom downstairs was filled with local and some national media. Chris was primping in the hallway and accepting congratulations from fellow officers. She hated the whole idea of the press conference, especially since her mind was like Swiss cheese. *What if they ask me how I cracked the case?* Could she tell them it was her gut instincts because, right now, that's all she could dredge up. She attempted to piece together the events of the last four days, but it was like putting together a jigsaw puzzle with twelve missing pieces. She remembered following Miles to Cath Bashir's home, but she couldn't understand why she did it. She recalled how she visualized the murder of Devinder Bashir with stunning accuracy, but she couldn't grasp how that was possible.

Something tugged on her memory—something safe and gentle. But every time she tried to grasp the feeling and give it dimension and meaning, it evaporated. *Jesus, the booze really is taking its toll.*

Turning to the window that looked down on 13th Street, she abruptly felt an uneasy clench in her gut. There was a little girl and there was darkness around her. And there was so much blood. But then the vision dissolved and she was numb and dead again, staring out the window and wondering how many inane questions she'd have to answer downstairs.

"They're ready for us, Jane." She turned to see Chris standing there. "You might want to fix your hair," he added.

Everything moved in slow motio,n as Jane reached inside her leather satchel and pulled out various items in an attempt to find a hairbrush. She felt around for the brush and, once locating it, had to disentangle it from her cell phone charger before pulling it out of the satchel. But there was something else stuck between the combs on the brush.

Lifting the brush out of the satchel, she found a single stick of incense. Somebody must have dropped it in my bag by mistake, she decided.

She wasn't sure why, but the sandalwood scent made her feel safe.